Nice Try, Tooth Fairy

Nice Try, Tooth Fairy

By Mary W. Olson

Illustrated by Katherine Tillotson

Pocket Books

London New York Sydney

POCKET
BOOKS

First published in Great Britain in 2003 by Pocket Books,

an imprint of Simon & Schuster UK Ltd

Originally published in the USA in 2000 by Simon & Schuster

Children's Publishing, New York

Text copyright © 2000 by Mary W. Olson

Illustrations copyright   © 2000 by Katherine Tillotson

A CIP catalogue record for this book is available from the British Library upon request.

ISBN 0-743-467949

Manufactured in China

1 3 5 7 9 10 8 6 4 2

To my husband, Doug, and my
two boys, Eric and Michael,
for all their love and support
—M. W. O.

To my parents,
Henry and Elizabeth
—K. T.

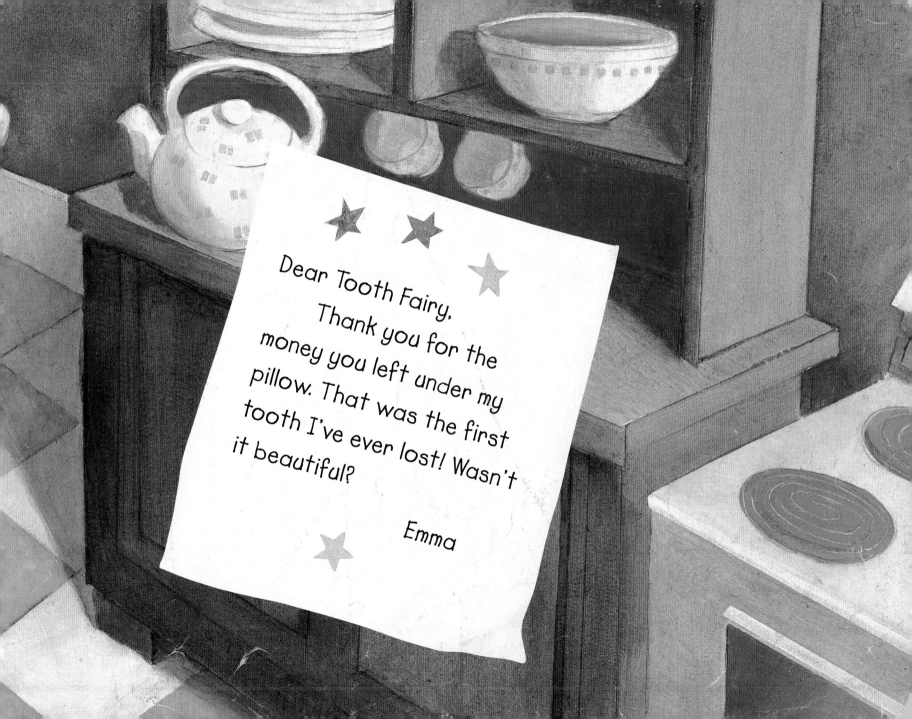

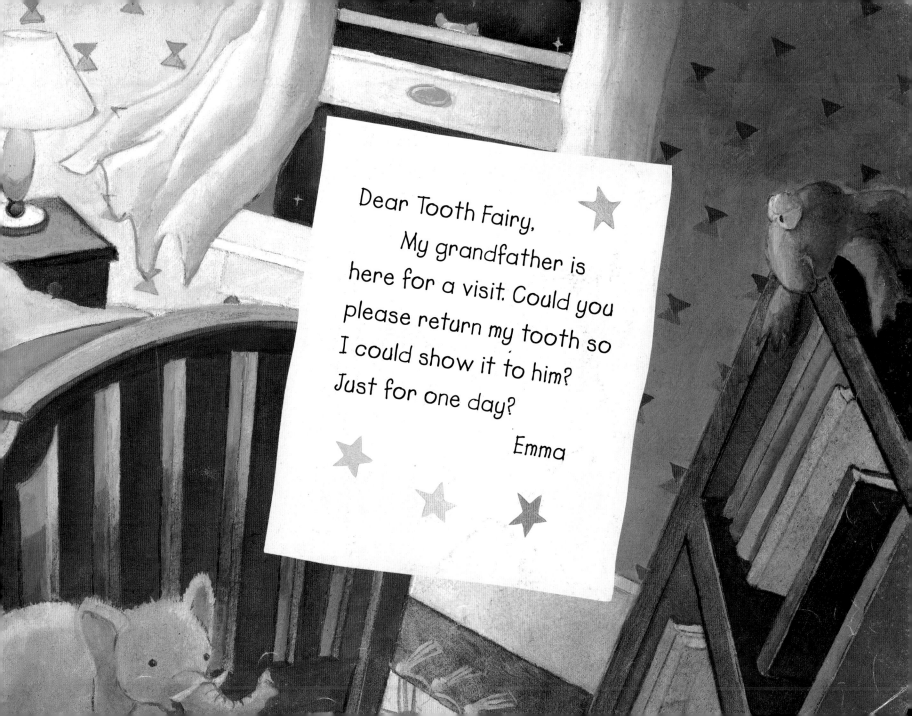

Dear Tooth Fairy,
    My mother says I should be pleased that you think I have such big teeth. But I think you made a mistake. Please can I have _my_ tooth back?

Emma

Dear Tooth Fairy,
    You don't have to worry about taking back that tooth. Last night I had a surprise visitor. That tooth fitted him just fine. Have you found my tooth yet?
                    Emma

Dear Tooth Fairy,
    No, my tooth isn't this small, either. I almost didn't see it under my pillow. Just as I was about to pick it up, a funny-looking creature tumbled through my window and grabbed it. I guess it was his.

    Emma

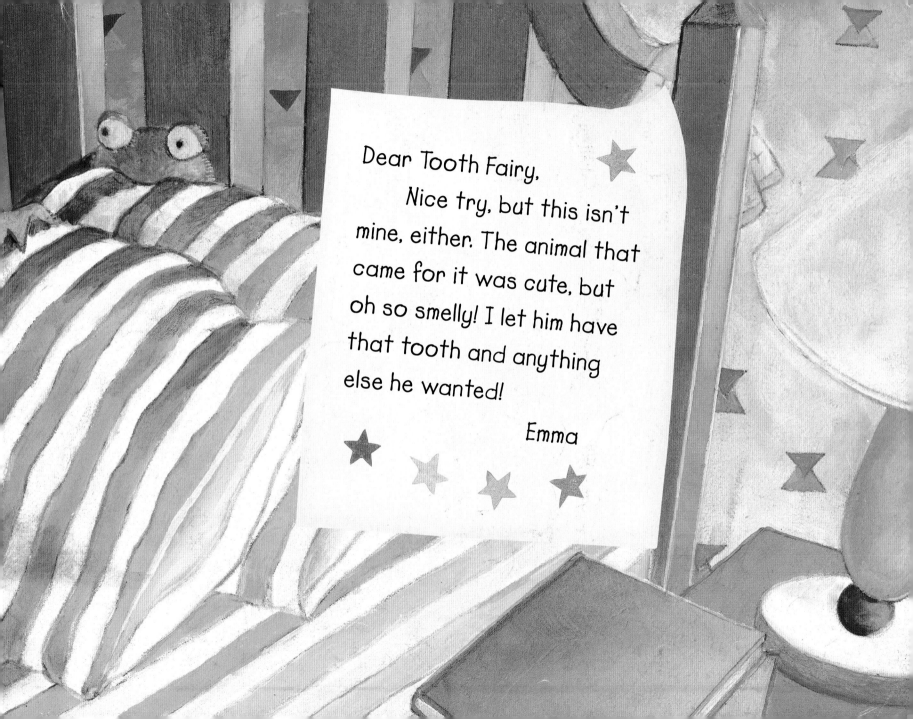

Dear Tooth Fairy,
    Nice try, but this isn't mine, either. The animal that came for it was cute, but oh so smelly! I let him have that tooth and anything else he wanted!

                        Emma

Dear Tooth Fairy,
    No, that tusk's not mine,
either. Not unless you think
I'm an elephant! And
speaking of elephants,
there's one trumpeting on
my front lawn now. Do you
think this might be his?

                    Emma

Dear Tooth Fairy,
    You sure must have a lot of teeth there. My mother says the tooth you left me last night is an alligator tooth. I'm looking for a place to put it so he'll be sure to find it!
    Here's a picture of my tooth, in case you've forgotten what it looked like.
                        Emma